The Scariest Stories You've Ever Heard

by Mark Mills

To Ryan and Marissa

Cover illustration by Richard Kriegler

Published by Willowisp Press, Inc.
10100 SBF Drive, Pinellas Park, Florida 34666

Printed in the United States of America

10 9 8 7 6 5 4 3

ISBN 0-87406-132-6

Introduction

You know the feeling. It's a pitch-black, spooky night. The moon is shining eerily through the mist. You hear a scuffling in the woods outside your house. It must be your imagination, you tell yourself. Then you hear a strange tapping at your window. You're just sure there's something out there—but what? You're too frightened to look and see—and too frightened not to. Slowly you creep to the window. The tapping is getting louder. Again, you're sure your imagination is playing tricks on you. You reach the window, and dare yourself to look out. You pull back the curtains and . . .

People have been frightening themselves like this for thousands of years. And they have been telling scary stories like the ones in this book for just as long. Because the stories have been told so many times, they tend to change just a little every time they are told. A few more details are added here and there so that they are just a little different—and scarier. But one thing is common to all of the stories— they have been told so many times that they sound as if they have really happened.

So, next time you are at a slumber party or

a camp-out or just feel like being scared, share these terrifying tales with your friends. Oh, you don't have to tell them exactly as they are written here. In fact, it's scarier if you don't. And you'll want to add your own details to make the stories sound really true. Any of these stories could be about someone you know—or used to know. Try telling them, but substituting someone you sound as if you know for the main character. It could be your long-lost cousin who takes a drive with his girlfriend one night in the hook story or your late great uncle who lives alone in the mountains with only a pack of dogs for company in the Taily-po story.

And remember, the way you tell the story is just as important as the story itself. Make sure the lights are turned down low. And talk slowly to build the tension. You might even want to act a little nervous, as if you are scared to find out the ending yourself.

So open the pages of this book—if you dare. Like whatever it is that is making the sound outside your window, there's something between these pages that's waiting, waiting for just the right time, just the right place to scare the living daylights out of you!

Tracey Dils, Editor

Contents

The Horrible Hook

THE evening was still warm when Jimmie and Suzanne left the movies. It was a perfect night to be out, and they were in no hurry to get home.

After picking up a snack, Jimmie suggested they go down to the lake. The young couple often drove there to enjoy the scenery, listen to the radio, or talk.

As they usually did, they parked the car alongside the gravel road in a spot that offered a great view. A light breeze blew through the open windows. Moonlight shimmered on the water, and a line of ducks floated by. Jimmie turned the radio on and found a station playing quiet music.

Suzanne sighed happily. She always enjoyed being here with Jimmie. He was one of the most popular boys in their high school, and captain of the basketball team as well, but he knew how to relax and enjoy the quiet of a spring evening.

After a few minutes, Jimmie broke the silence to ask Suzanne about their plans for the prom next month. As she turned to answer him, Suzanne suddenly felt a strange and overpowering uneasiness.

"Jimmie, something's wrong," she said slowly.

"Wrong?" he asked, looking surprised. "Is something wrong about the prom? After we've been looking forward to it for so long?"

"No, not the prom. Something else. Right now. Something doesn't feel right in this place."

Jimmie looked around and shrugged. "I don't see anything different. You're imagining things."

Suzanne peered out of the car into the darkness. The strange feeling wouldn't go away. "Listen, do you hear anything?"

Jimmie gave her a funny look. "What's the matter with you?"

"Just listen, would you?"

Suzanne turned off the radio and they both sat silently, scarcely breathing. After a few moments, Jimmie turned the radio back on and said, "I don't hear a thing. I think your imagination is working overtime."

Suzanne quickly turned the radio off again. "Jimmie Morrow, that's my point. It's too quiet. I don't hear the ducks or birds or crickets or anything. This place is giving me the creeps." She immediately felt chilled and rubbed her arms, looking away from him.

Jimmie grinned patiently and touched her arm. "Hey, it's okay. Are you cold? Roll up your window, and put my jacket on."

They rolled up the car windows and settled back in their seats. "You're probably right," Suzanne said. "But I felt so weird, and I don't know why . . ."

A few minutes passed without a word. Then suddenly, Suzanne stiffened and sat bolt upright again. "Jimmie!" Her voice held a note of near panic. "Please, let's get out of here! I am absolutely sure there's—"

But Jimmie was holding up his hand for silence. The radio station had interrupted its music for a special bulletin.

". . . escaped from the Millerton Asylum for the Criminally Insane early this evening. Convicted five years ago of committing a series of murders, he is considered emotionally unstable and extremely dangerous. Johnson uses a hook on his right arm, as a replacement for the hand he lost in a train accident several years ago."

9

Suzanne glanced nervously at Jimmie, who shrugged as if the report wasn't as important as he had expected. He started to turn the radio dial, but Suzanne shoved his hand away.

"The state police have set up roadblocks in the surrounding areas," the announcer continued, "and a massive manhunt is underway. Anyone in possession of information concerning the whereabouts of Johnson should get in touch immediately with the county sheriff's office. And now back to our regular programming."

"Jimmie, we've got to get out of here!" Suzanne pleaded. "That prison is only a few miles away from here!"

"Geez, Suzie, relax. That guy wouldn't come this way. An escapee would head north toward the interstate highway."

But Suzanne was getting angry. "Jimmie, I want to go home."

"Suzie, don't make me mad. I'm telling you, there's nothing to worry about!"

"Jimmie, take me home—NOW!"

"Okay," Jimmie sputtered. "If that's the way you want it." Angrily, he turned the key in the ignition and shoved the gas pedal to the floor. The car fishtailed in the loose gravel, sending pebbles high in the air behind it.

Suzanne huddled in misery against the car

door. Jimmie stared ahead at the road in stony silence. In 15 minutes, they were home.

Still angry, Jimmie screeched the car to a halt in Suzanne's drive and jumped out. He headed for Suzanne's side of the car, but she clambered out by herself and slammed the door behind her.

In that moment, both teenagers froze. Staring at the car door, Suzanne slowly started to shriek in horror, and Jimmie felt every muscle go tight. Hanging on the handle of the car door was a razor-sharp, bloody hook!

Never Walk There at Night

IT was getting late. The slumber party at Annie's house was growing quiet. As midnight approached, one of the girls began to tell a ghost story. Someone else turned the lights down low, and all sorts of scary stories were exchanged.

"You know, our house is only a block away from the cemetery," said Annie. "You wouldn't believe some of the things I've seen while looking out my window."

A few of the girls giggled, but Annie looked serious as she continued. "My grandmother told me never to walk in the cemetery at night. She said if you step on a grave, the person underneath will grab you and try to pull you under. And then you'll be dead, too."

"Oh, that's just an old wives' tale," scoffed Diane. "The cemetery doesn't scare me."

"If you're so brave, why don't you go over

there right now?" Jo Ann dared her.

"What for? It wouldn't prove anything," said Diane.

"It would just prove that you aren't the scaredy-cat we all know you are," replied Annie.

"Scaredy-cat, scaredy-cat, Diane is a scaredy-cat," sang all the girls. Diane tried to shush them, but they kept on taunting her.

As the girls' teasing grew more insistent, Diane finally blurted out, "Okay, I'll do it!"

The other girls clapped their hands in excitement. Annie went over to the window of her second-story room and looked outside. "Darn, the leaves on the trees hide the view of the cemetery," she said. "You'll have to leave a sign to show that you really were there, so we'll know you didn't cheat."

Annie glanced about her room. She went over to her desk and grabbed an old letter opener from the pencil cup.

"Here, Diane. Take this letter opener. When you get inside the cemetery, go stand on a grave and stick it in the ground. Then we'll all go get it in the morning. If it's there, we'll know you really aren't a scaredy-cat."

Diane took the letter opener and the girls escorted her to the front door. "See you soon, Diane," said Annie, as she closed the door.

"Unless the boogeyman gets you!"

The night was warm, but very windy. Diane wished she had put on a coat or bathrobe over her long nightgown. But she knew the cemetery was only a block away. She could whisk over there and back in no time.

As she came up to the cemetery gates, Diane walked more slowly. "I've got nothing to worry about," she said to herself. "There are no such things as ghosts."

Inside the iron gates, Diane looked around. The only noise she heard was the rustle of leaves in the trees. Clouds passed in the sky, causing moon shadows to dance on the tombstones. Filled with an eerie feeling, she pressed on into the old graveyard.

Holding her breath and trying to calm her pounding heart, Diane picked out an old grave and stood on it. Then she bent over, grasped the letter opener, and plunged it deep into the ground.

The job was done! But as she straightened up to leave, Diane felt something tugging at her nightgown. She pulled, but she couldn't free herself! She was trapped! As she struggled against the firm hold on her nightgown, she gave in to all the terror that had been building up inside her. Her horrible scream might have been heard at the house a block away, but the wind carried it off into the night.

Annie looked out her window toward the cemetery. She strained to see, but the trees blocked her view. One of the girls mentioned that Diane had been gone almost an hour.

"We'd better go see what's happened to her," said Annie, beginning to worry about her friend. The girls all put on their bathrobes and shoes, and walked as a group to the cemetery.

There they found Diane, sprawled before a crumbling tombstone. Having accidentally stuck the letter opener through the hem of her own nightgown, she had pinned herself to the grave. So terrified was she by the thought of death's grasp, she had simply died of fright.

A Deadly Night at the Dew Drop Inn

THE wipers on the car couldn't go fast enough to clear away the torrent of water on the windshield.

Sam hunched over the steering wheel, straining to see the road. But his headlights only reflected the rain pouring down in front of them.

What a horrible night to be out, he thought. *At least there's nobody else crazy enough to be driving on this mountain road.*

But as Sam rounded a curve, terror shot through him as he realized he was wrong. Just ahead were two sets of headlights, side by side, advancing fast. A car passing a truck? On a curve? In this weather?

Sam braked wildly and tried to avoid the oncoming vehicles, but there was nowhere to turn. At the last moment he ducked down, covering his head with his arms.

The crash was like an explosion. Glass flew everywhere, and steel bent with a sickening sound. Then as quickly as it had happened, it was over.

Sam slowly opened his eyes and looked around. Rain beat upon his face through the broken windshield. The car was totally demolished, but Sam realized with amazement that he was all right. The steering wheel was pushing against his chest, but he managed to wriggle free. Twisting around carefully, Sam climbed out of the car through the windshield.

The hood of the car was crumpled up like an accordion. It was smashed against a huge boulder to the side of the road. The car and the truck that had caused the accident were nowhere in sight.

Sam slid off the car into the mud, rain continuing to pour down on him. He looked up and down the road.

What could have happened to them? he wondered. *Seems like at least one of them would have stopped to see if I was okay.*

Across the highway shone the lights from a small building, a roadside tavern. Through the rain Sam could dimly make out a sign. The place was called the Dew Drop Inn.

He started immediately toward the inn.

Lucky for me, Sam thought. *At least I'll be able to dry off and call for help. I could have been stuck here for hours.*

When he reached the door of the inn, he could hear the strains of a popular country song playing on the jukebox. Ducking inside, Sam shook the rain off his jacket. The place was full of people seated at tables, dancing, and milling around. Loud conversation and laughter added to the noise of the music.

That's strange, thought Sam as he viewed the scene. *There weren't any cars out front. They must all be parked out back.*

He spied the bartender, who greeted Sam with a toothy smile as he wound his way through the tables to the bar. "Howdy, friend. What can I get you?"

"Do you have a phone I can use?"

"I've got a phone," said the bartender. "But you can't use it."

Sam looked bewildered.

The bartender smiled again. "The lines are down. Didn't you notice the storm?"

"Sure did," said Sam, not very amused. "Listen, I just had a wreck and totaled my car. Some people are expecting me in the city."

The bartender continued to smile as if he hadn't heard Sam's bad news. "Gee, fella, I'm sorry about that. But you're not going anywhere in this storm. Sit down and make yourself comfortable. The folks in here are real friendly."

An attractive young woman suddenly appeared at Sam's shoulder. "Sit down at the table over here," she said. "You look tired."

He nodded in agreement. He was tired, and he felt very shaken by the accident. *Besides,* he thought, *the bartender was probably right— there was nothing he could do at the moment.* As he took off his jacket, he noticed it was already dry, as were his pants and shoes.

"How in the world did that happen?" he muttered to himself. "I was soaked when I walked in here."

The young woman brought him a sandwich and a cup of coffee. She sat down with him and asked him why he was traveling on such a stormy night. Sam answered her briefly as he looked more closely at his surroundings. The tavern seemed old, but was not run-down. Several couples were shuffling their feet to the music from the jukebox. Others were talking in groups of threes and fours. At least two card games were in progress.

As he stared, a man looked up from one of the card games and motioned to Sam. "Do you want to play cards?" he called. "We've been saving a place just for you. In fact, we've already dealt you in."

Sam looked at the vacant chair the man was waving him toward. *Sure, why not?* he thought. *I've got nothing better to do.* He moved to the crowded table and swept up the pile of cards at his place. "What are we playing?"

* * * * *

Sam's eyes fluttered open. He groggily thought back to the night before and tried to remember where he was. Slowly it all came back—the accident, the tavern, the card game. He lifted his head from the table where he was slumped and he looked around.

Wait a minute, he thought in confusion. *What's happened to this place?*

Cobwebs were everywhere, and a thick coat of dust covered the room. It looked as if no one had set foot inside the inn for years.

Sunlight streamed through the window. Voices could be heard outside. Stretching his stiff joints, Sam made his way to the window. What he saw chilled him to the bone.

Beside the wreckage of his car were an ambulance and two police cruisers. The ambulance attendants were placing a body on a stretcher. Then they covered it with a blanket, pulling it up over the head. As they slid the stretcher into the ambulance, a patrolman uncovered the face for just a moment. Sam recognized himself.

Letting out a shriek of terror, Sam pounded on the glass. But his fist made no sound as it made contact, and the windowpane didn't even rattle.

"The poor guy didn't have a chance," one of the patrolmen said. "His chest was crushed by the steering wheel."

A medic came over to the policeman. "I don't know why we don't just wait here on those stormy nights," he said. "There must have been at least 40 people killed smashing into that boulder over the last 20 years."

Sam felt the horrible truth start to wash over him. Could it be that he was . . . *dead*?

The men outside looked toward the tavern. "Ever since the Dew Drop closed, there's been one accident after another," said the other patrolman. "Come on, let's get out of here."

Panic-stricken, Sam ran to open the door, but the handle wouldn't turn. He pounded on the door, but again there was no sound.

A familiar voice came from the back of the tavern.

"Settle down, neighbor. Like I told you last night, you're not going anywhere."

Sam turned around and recognized the bartender's toothy grin. The figure standing behind the bar, cleaning a glass, was a smiling skeleton!

The Hand

ALEX was the most unpopular student in medical school. It wasn't because he was mean, or unkind, or unfriendly. In fact, he was just the opposite.

Most of the other students had to work hard and struggle to pass exams. Not Alex. He always knew the right answer when called upon in lectures. He always could diagnose a patient's health problem. His lab work was always perfect.

And that's why everyone hated Alex. The other medical students were jealous. It was as simple as that. Alex's reputation continued to grow. Over the long semesters of grueling study, the doctors and professors loved making Alex an example of how to do things right. Of course, this just made the other students resent him all the more.

Finally, one of the students, Bart, could take

it no longer. He called a meeting of some of his classmates.

"I'm sick and tired of hearing Alex this and Alex that," Bart said to his friends as they sat around the table. The room was dark except for a single light, hanging low over the table. "We've got to do something."

"Bart, you're just jealous," said Cindy, a young woman ranked high in the class. "I'm getting good grades, too. How do I know you won't turn against me next?"

"Bart's right, Cindy," said Tom. "It's one thing to get good grades, like you do. But Alex is so perfect, it's . . . it's . . . unnatural. It's as if he isn't human!"

Cindy giggled. "Tom, you've been watching too many late-night movies."

"It's not funny," said Bart. "He makes me sick. You never see him anywhere but in class, or the library, or his dorm room. I don't even see him eat. He doesn't go to parties or do anything with other students."

"But you can't say he isn't friendly," countered Cindy. "He always says hello. And I know he pointed out a mistake on your term paper, Tom, when you were studying beside him in the library. You needed a good grade, and he was willing to help you."

"Yeah, but he shouldn't have been so happy

to do it," said Tom.

The group sat silent. The last of the four, sitting in silence until then, turned his face up into the light. "We can find out if Alex is human, and teach him a lesson, too," said Derek. "I have an idea."

Big and tall, Derek had played football as an undergraduate, and he was well-known at the university. He was a leader—his size alone commanded respect. When he spoke, people listened.

So now, the group paid close attention as he told them his plan.

* * * * *

"Did you get it?" whispered Tom outside the anatomy lab. Only the dim red light of the exit sign shone down in the darkened hall.

"Yeah, it's in here," said Bart, pointing to his athletic bag. "Let's get out of here. Derek will be waiting for us."

Inside the lab, a lone cadaver lay on the autopsy table. Its right arm, hidden under the sheet, ended at the wrist in a grisly stump.

* * * * *

"I can't believe you guys are going through

with this," said Cindy. "You're crazy, you know that?"

Derek ignored Cindy's comment. He smiled as he peeked into the bag. "This is great. Alex is going to love this," he said to no one in particular. Bart and Tom patted each other on the back.

"You guys are *really* crazy," repeated Cindy. "I don't want to know anything about this. I'm leaving."

"Aw, c'mon, Cindy. Don't be a spoilsport," said Tom.

"Cindy, it's not like the hand belongs to anybody," added Bart. "I mean, the bodies we cut up are convicts who died in prison. Nobody claimed them—who would want them?"

Cindy looked angry. "It's not right," she said. "I hope you guys get caught!" She headed for the door.

"Cindy!" barked Derek. "Don't ever say a word of this to anyone. You understand?"

She nodded, then slipped out the door.

Derek smiled. "Men, we're about to have a little fun."

* * * * *

When the trio got to Alex's room, he was

there, as usual, studying. Alex was surprised to see three of his classmates at his door. He rarely had visitors.

"Alex, we're having a real problem with Dr. King's assignment," said Bart. "We know you could help us. Would you come to the study table downstairs?"

Alex didn't say anything at first. This request was truly unusual. Then Tom spoke up. "Say yes, Alex! We really need your help."

"Okay," said Alex. A smile broke on his face. "Just let me get my books."

Downstairs, the group plopped down at the study table and spread out their books and papers. Alex immediately began explaining the assignment, but the guys only pretended to listen. After a few minutes, Derek excused himself. "I just remembered I've got to call my girlfriend," he said. "I'll be right back."

Derek walked toward the telephone booth, then ducked into the rest room. Behind the door was the athletic bag, just where he had left it. He grabbed it and headed for the back stairs.

When he reached Alex's floor, he peeked through the window in the stairwell door. The hall was empty. Walking deliberately, he made his way to Alex's room and pushed the door open.

What a geek, thought Derek, noticing that Alex's room was perfection, too. The bed was made. Books were lined perfectly on their shelves. Not a sheet of paper was out of place. No pictures or posters decorated the wall. *It's no wonder the guy has a private room,* thought Derek. *Nobody else could live like this!*

Opening the closet door, Derek pulled the string on the light in the dark enclosure. He wasn't surprised to find all Alex's clothes hanging perfectly, too.

So far, all was going according to plan. Derek reached into the bag and pulled out the bloody hand, which he had wrapped in plastic. He put on a pair of surgical gloves and unwrapped the hand. In a few moments he had tied the string of the closet light around the hand's wrist.

Derek smiled to himself. *I'd love to see the look on Alex's face when he grabs the hand to turn on the light,* he thought.

Packing up quickly, Derek closed the closet door. He checked the hallway, then slipped quietly back down the stairs to rejoin the study group. As he sat down, he gave everyone a thumbs-up sign. Alex thought it meant that everything was okay with Derek's girlfriend, but Tom and Bart knew otherwise.

* * * *

The next morning, Tom, Bart, and Derek were waiting for Alex outside the lecture hall. They were laughing about their plot against Alex when Cindy walked up to them.

"Did you hotshots have your fun?" she asked.

They proceeded to tell her the whole story. "It went like clockwork," said Derek as he finished the tale. "We're waiting to see Alex's face now."

"I know one thing," said Cindy. "I heard there's going to be an investigation at the anatomy lab. It seems the hand you guys snatched belonged to a notorious strangler. Some sicko newspaper reporter came in and wanted pictures of the guy's hands, and that's when they discovered one of the hands was missing."

Derek laughed. "They can't prove anything on us. In fact, they'll probably think Alex took it. This is even better!"

The bell rang. Alex was nowhere in sight. The students gave one last look down the hall, and then found their seats in class.

All day the group watched to see when Alex would turn up. But he didn't appear. What made it especially strange was that Alex had never missed class before.

That evening, Derek could stand the suspense no more. He called Bart on the phone. "You get Tom and meet me at Alex's room in half an hour. This is getting weird."

The three pranksters snickered like first-graders when they knocked on Alex's door. But they quieted down when no one answered after the third and fourth knocks.

"He must be out," said Bart. "Let's go." He sounded a little nervous.

Derek turned the doorknob. The door swung open. "Let's see if the hand is still there," he said.

The three crept over toward the closet. The door was slightly ajar. Pulling it open, the boys gasped in pure horror. The hand still hung from the string, but now its muscles were strained in a death grip. Clenched tightly within its massive fingers was Alex's whitened throat. Limp and lifeless, his body swayed before them in the strangler's cruel caress.

The Horror in
the Backseat

IT was nearly midnight when Linda made a mad dash to her car in the pouring rain. The school parking lot was nearly empty. She was one of the last students to leave. Tomorrow was the annual high school musical, and she had just finished painting the last of the scenery.

Lightning flashed close by, momentarily replacing night with day. The thunder shook her car.

Bad storm, she thought. She couldn't wait to get home and into her bed. The stage crew had worked extremely hard the last few days, and she was exhausted.

Turning onto the highway, Linda drove slowly in spite of her desire to get home. The rain was coming down hard. Lightning flashed again, and then streetlights went out. Only the beams from her headlights lit the road ahead.

Behind her she noticed another vehicle approaching, the only other car on the road. As it pulled up close to her car, its lights flashed, as if signaling to pass. Linda couldn't imagine anyone trying to pass on this rainy, wet road, but she slowed a little to let the car by.

But the car stayed right behind her. Suddenly, the headlights flashed again. Then the driver pulled his vehicle up right behind the rear bumper of Linda's car.

She could tell now it wasn't a car, but a pickup truck. She slowed her car again, and edged to the far right side of the lane, but the pickup wouldn't pass. It stayed close behind her. Dangerously close.

Is this guy crazy? Linda thought. *Or is he deliberately following me?* She glanced uneasily up and down the wet road. No one else was in sight. The truck clung behind her, just inches between them.

Turning down another street, Linda grew more concerned as the pickup stayed close. The truck's bright lights came on again. Linda decided to increase her speed, despite the rain.

She turned down another street and sped through a red light, but the pickup kept pace. She pushed the accelerator down even more.

Although the truck dropped back slightly, its unseen driver flashed its lights several times in a row.

Now Linda was getting scared. *What's that guy want?* she thought. She tried to lose the truck by cutting across the pavement of a corner gas station, but the driver seemed to be able to tell every move she would make. He hung on doggedly.

Racing toward her parents' home outside of town, Linda felt the car sliding on the wet pavement. She knew she was driving too fast. Still the pickup bore down on her, lights flashing.

Up ahead Linda saw the driveway to her house. She turned sharply, almost skidding into the ditch, and started blowing the car horn frantically. The truck turned in right behind her. Still pushing on the horn, Linda screeched to a halt and then jumped out of the car.

Linda's father ran out on the front porch, alarmed by the sound of the horn. As his frightened daughter ran into his arms, the driver of the truck got out and pulled a rifle down from the gun rack in the cab.

"Daddy," she sobbed, "that man has been following me."

"Hold it, mister," yelled her father. "I'm

calling the police."

"Well, sir, you do that," said the truck driver, standing in the rain next to Linda's car. He clutched his rifle and looked down through the car window. "I think they'd be real interested in my story."

"Now, just what do you mean by that?" Linda's father snapped. He had untangled himself from his daughter's arms and now was striding angrily toward the stranger.

The man jerked his thumb toward the car window. "Have a look," he said. "My car horn doesn't work. So flashing my lights was the only way I could help that girl."

Linda's father peered into the darkened car. His expression changed from curiosity to horror. He looked back at the stranger, speechless.

"Yes," the man said, answering the unasked question. "He'd duck down every time those high beams hit him. I stayed on that car so close, I could see him every time he started to raise up."

Linda could bear the suspense no longer. Moving slowly down the porch steps and across the drive, she approached the car in fear and fascination.

"Young lady," said the man, "I'm right glad I came up behind you."

Linda now could see why. Her insides ran cold as she glanced in the window. There, cringing on the floor of the car, was a huge man with a murderous look on his face. In his hand was a gleaming hatchet!

The Baby-sitter

THE doctor's house looked huge from the street, but it seemed even bigger inside. Jennifer's father had told her that the doctor and his wife had spent a lot of money fixing up the old three-story mansion. And it showed.

Dr. Phillips gave her a quick tour of the house, while his wife finished getting ready to go out. Their two children, Andy and Abbey, tagged along, giggling and laughing.

Jennifer was impressed. The rooms were so spacious—and so many of them! The doctor even had a huge office and library on the third floor.

The little tour group ended up in the foyer. "Jennifer, I'm glad you could baby-sit for us tonight," said Dr. Phillips, "especially on such short notice. We've heard some good things about you."

"Thank you," said Jennifer. "I'm sure Andy

and Abbey will be fine with me."

Just then Mrs. Phillips appeared, gliding down the stairs. "Jennie, I wrote everything down and taped it to the refrigerator door," she said. "The phone number where you can reach us, emergency numbers, and the number for my husband's pager. Snacks are in the refrigerator, you can make popcorn in the microwave, the kids are to be in bed by 8:30, Andy needs to—"

"Jane," interrupted Dr. Phillips, "Jennifer can read. We'd better get going."

His wife smiled. "You're right. Jennie, we'll be home about midnight and then we'll drive you home."

She bent over and kissed her children. "Be good," she said as she and her husband left the house.

"Hooray," yelled the kids when the car disappeared down the driveway. Nine-year-old Andy ran into the family room and jammed a tape into the video player. His five-year-old sister grabbed Jennifer's hand and took her to see her dolls.

Eventually, Jennifer was able to steer Abbey into the kitchen. The baby-sitter read the list Mrs. Phillips had left, and got a package of cookies and some milk. "Come on," she said to Abbey. "Let's take this stuff into the family room and watch TV with Andy."

When the videotape was over, it was almost 8:30.

"Okay, kids, it's time to get ready for bed," said Jennifer. Abbey was already sleepy, but Jennifer was surprised when even Andy willingly agreed. "All right," he said. "I'll race you upstairs."

It didn't take long for the children to get undressed and washed. Abbey gave Jennifer a kiss and quickly fell asleep in her big, four-poster bed. Jennifer went to Andy's room to check on him.

The boy was standing by a low counter that ran nearly the entire length of the wall. It was filled with all kinds of electronic gear—a tape deck and stereo, a computer and keyboard, and several other pieces of equipment she didn't recognize. Andy was adjusting the dials on one of them.

"Neat, huh?" he said when he noticed how impressed she looked by all the devices.

Jennifer nodded.

"My dad's really a scientist," the boy continued. "He does medical research. He just sees patients and operates to make a living, but he likes doing experiments more. He's got a lab in the basement, but we're not allowed down there. Blood samples and stuff."

"That's great, Andy," said Jennifer. "But now it's time to go to bed. You can tell me more some other time."

Andy crawled into bed and grabbed a comic book off the nightstand. "I'm going to read this and then I'll go to sleep. Good night, Jennie."

Jennifer turned and closed the door behind her. A ray of light peeked out into the hall from under Andy's door.

Tiptoeing downstairs, Jennifer headed for the refrigerator and picked out a red, juicy apple. Then she spread her homework out on the kitchen table and started to work.

She'd only been at it a few minutes when the phone rang. *It must be Mrs. Phillips, checking up on things,* she thought as she reached for the kitchen extension. "Hello?"

The line was silent. Then she heard a click and a dial tone.

"Wrong number," Jennifer said to herself. She heard the grandfather clock in the sitting room chime nine.

Wondering whether the phone had awakened the children, she went upstairs. The light was out in Andy's room. Abbey was still fast asleep. She went back downstairs to do more homework.

As the old clock chimed the half hour, the

telephone rang again. This time Jennifer heard heavy breathing on the other end of the line.

"Who is this?" she asked.

The breathing continued, but there was no reply. Quicky she hung up the receiver.

Creep, she thought. She tried to go back to her homework, but she couldn't concentrate. The calls had unnerved her.

Wandering back into the family room, Jennifer turned on the TV.

As the network changed shows, the phone rang once again. It was 10:00 P.M. Jennifer didn't want to answer, but the note from Mrs. Phillips had said that the medical bureau might call. Jennifer would then have to notify the doctor if he was needed at the hospital.

After several rings, she grabbed the phone. "Hello?"

Heavy breathing.

"Hello? What do you want?"

A strange, eerie voice answered slowly. "I'm coming to get you. Just one more hour."

Click. The caller hung up.

Panicked, Jennifer sat staring at the receiver, wondering what to do. Finally she decided to call the operator.

The woman's voice was reassuring. "We'll set up a trace on your line. What's the number? You said the caller has phoned every half hour? Okay, it will take about that long to set up the trace. Now, you have to keep the caller on the line next time so we have time to get a trace. I'll call you right back after you hang up."

Jennifer felt a little relieved. But as it got closer to 10:30 P.M., her anxiety grew. She watched the minutes slowly tick off her watch. The grandfather clock chimed the half hour. Nothing.

Just when she had decided no one would call, the phone rang again. Jennifer's head started to pound.

"Who is this?" asked Jennifer. She could barely hold the receiver. "I want to talk to you."

The mysterious voice answered, "I'm coming to get you. Just 30 more minutes."

"Wait! Why are you coming?"

There was an ominous pause. "To kill you, of course."

Jennifer heard herself shriek, but she didn't dare hang up the receiver yet. Would the operator have had time to trace the call?

"Don't hang up," Jennifer stammered, barely able to get the words out. "Why do you want me?"

"I'm coming to get you. Just 30 more

minutes, and I'll be there."

Jennifer tried to stall for more time. "But why me? How do you know me? I don't know who you are!"

"Yes, you do," said the voice, which sounded as if it were not human. "And I know you."

She couldn't bear it any longer. "Just leave me alone. Leave me alone!" she yelled.

The caller hung up.

No sooner had Jennifer set the receiver down than the phone rang again. It was the operator. Her voice was no longer calm.

"Get out of the house, fast," she said. "I'm calling the police. The calls are coming from the other line inside your house!"

Jennifer dropped the phone, horrified, and ran for the stairs. Her only thought was to get the kids and escape from this house before—

"Jennie, what's wrong? Noises woke me up." It was Abbey, who was standing at the top of the stairs rubbing her eyes.

Taking two steps at a time, Jennifer dashed up the stairs, calling for Andy. "Stay right there!" she told Abbey frantically. "I'll be right back!" Racing wildly for Andy's room, she jerked open his door and flicked on the light.

She could only scream in terror at what she saw. Andy wasn't in the rumpled bed, and the sheets were stained with blood!

Running back to the stairs, she grabbed Abbey around the waist, ran downstairs and out the front door. As she and the little girl reached the sidewalk, two police cruisers screeched to a stop, their lights flashing red and blue.

Breathless, Jennifer pointed to the house. "Inside! Upstairs! Blood all over Andy's bed! And I don't know where he is!" Weapons drawn, the police entered the house. They stormed through the second story, then raced to the third. Flinging open the door to Dr. Phillips' office, they came face to face with the culprit.

He was sitting at the desk by the telephone, toying with an electronic voice-changer. Blood was on his hands. Lying on the desk was a laboratory blood bag, emptied of its contents.

When the police entered the room, he gave them a devilish grin. "I really scared her, huh?" said Andy.

Prom Fright!

"I think it's out of gas," said Josh. He turned to Sarah and grinned sheepishly. "Honest."

Sarah frowned. "Can't you check the engine or something to be sure?"

"Yeah, okay. But I'm sure we're out of gas."

Josh got out of the car, popped the hood, and disappeared under the raised expanse of metal.

How could this be happening? thought Sarah. *And on prom night, too.*

So far, this evening had been everything she had ever dreamed of. Her dress was perfect—everybody at the dance had complimented her on it. And her date, Josh, was the most popular boy in school. He looked great in his tux, and he had even rented this limousine for the evening.

Now they were on their way to an after-prom party at an exclusive country club several miles outside town. *But now this!* Sarah thought. *It'll ruin everything.*

"Josh, we're going to be late," called Sarah. "Can't you get it started?"

The boy got back in the car and tried the key again. The car still wouldn't start. "Look," he said, "the gas gauge reads empty."

Sarah was getting angry. "Well, didn't you notice that when you picked it up this afternoon?"

"Yeah, but I thought the gauge was broken. They told me the tank is always full when a car goes out, and I'm supposed to make sure it's filled when I bring it back."

The couple sat in silence, both staring into the night. Suddenly Josh sat up straight, opened the car door, and jumped out.

"Wait!" Sarah called, instantly alert. "You're not going to leave me here, are you?"

Josh peered back into the car. "I'm just going to look in the trunk to see if there's a gas can."

In a few minutes he returned, empty-handed. "Nothing," he said. "I guess I'll have to find a gas station."

"Josh, you can't leave me here alone!" Sarah was beginning to sound panicky. "Didn't you hear about the maniac on the loose?"

"Sarah those news reports about the lunatic are exaggerated. Besides, you'll be safe here in the car. You can't walk anywhere in those spike-heeled shoes, that's for sure. I can go faster alone anyway. That way we won't miss much of the party."

"But Josh, we were one of the last couples to leave the prom. Everybody else will be there already."

"I'm sorry, but I can't get us there without gas," said Josh. "There was a service station by the turnoff about a mile back. I'll run down there and get a ride back."

"I'm scared. Don't leave me."

"You'll be okay. Just keep the doors locked. Wait, I've got an idea." Josh returned to the trunk and came back with a blanket.

"Here," he said, offering her the blanket. "Lie down in the back and put this blanket over you. If anybody passes the car, they'll think it's deserted. Nobody will bother you. Keep the doors locked and you'll be safe."

Sarah could see she didn't have much of a choice. Josh was right—the shoes she had on certainly weren't made for trudging down gravel roads in the night.

"How will I know it's you when you're back?" she asked.

"I'll knock on the hood of the car three

times. Then you'll know it's me."

"Well, all right. But please hurry. And be careful."

Josh gave her a quick smile and a wave, and then disappeared into the darkness.

Sarah crawled into the backseat with the blanket. According to the clock on the dashboard, it was after 1:00 A.M. Glancing out the car windows, she realized how alone she was. With no moonlight, the night was especially dark. No houses could be seen anywhere.

The limo sat under a huge oak tree at the edge of the woods. On the other side of the road was an open field.

Sarah made sure all the doors were locked, then ducked under the blanket, hoping Josh would return soon. After a while, her eyes slowly closed and she drifted off to sleep.

Thump.

Sarah gave a frightened gasp as she awoke. Then she realized it must be Josh.

Thump, thump.

Relieved, Sarah started to pull the blanket off her head.

Thump, thump.

A wave of fear again rushed over her. She felt paralyzed. *Didn't Josh say three knocks?* Sarah thought. Her mind raced. Should she call out to see if it was Josh? What if it wasn't him? If it was him, she decided, he'd call her name. She lay perfectly still.

Thump, thump . . . thump . . . thump.

Now Sarah was certain it wasn't Josh. Her heart was pounding and she was suddenly short of breath. Someone was knocking on the hood of the car. Could it be the escaped maniac? If it was, why would he be knocking on the hood of a parked car?

For what seemed like hours, the irregular thumping shook the car's hood. Sarah was so tense that her muscles screamed in pain. But she dared not move.

Finally, she heard another car approaching. It stopped somewhere behind the disabled vehicle. Then, even through the blanket, she could tell that a bright light was being passed over the limo.

A loudspeaker blared out in the night, and she nearly jumped off the car seat. "This is the police. Is anybody in that car?"

Sarah wanted to scream, but her throat was so dry she couldn't make a sound.

"I repeat, this is the police. Is anybody in that car?"

Sarah slowly sat up and looked out the back window. The brilliance of the searchlight blinded her. She tried to shield her eyes.

The voice behind the light called, "Miss, are you all right?"

Sarah nodded her head, still trying to find her voice.

"Okay, I want you to get out of the car and walk this way. Walk directly toward this light. Do not look behind you. Whatever you do, *do not* look behind you. All right?"

Sarah unlocked the door and stepped outside. Her legs were so stiff she could barely move, and she wobbled on her high-heeled shoes. Swallowing hard, she took a few hesitant steps toward the light.

"You're doing fine, Miss. Come this way. Remember, don't turn around."

As she moved forward, Sarah began to gather her wits. *What's going on?* she thought. *Where's Josh? Why can't I turn around?*

She could make out the police car now, and the two policemen standing behind the cruiser's open door. One of the men had his arms outstretched to her.

But Sarah could no longer stand the suspense. She threw a glance back at the limo, then froze, riveted by what she saw. The scream that had been building inside her broke forth.

Above the limo was Josh, hanging from a noose tied to a limb of the old oak tree. His legs dangled freely, swaying in the breeze. His lifeless feet were hitting the hood of the car.

Thump, thump.

The Night of the Sasquatch

IN the mountain wilderness of Idaho, a group of Boy Scouts was on its annual winter camp-out.

The trip was to last five days. They would hike for two days into the snowy wilderness, stay a third day at a remote cabin, and then start the journey back. Only the best Scouts could be allowed to make the trip. Each fall the boys who wanted to go on the camp-out had to pass a rigorous wilderness survival test.

Leading the group was an Indian named Katooni, a member of the Nez Percé tribe. An expert on the wilderness, Katooni was the descendant of people who had lived here long before the white man had come. He knew all the stories and legends about the mountains. Many Scouts made the long trip just to listen to Katooni tell his tales.

After two full days of hiking and an overnight stay in pup tents, the Scouts reached the remote cabin. To the weary boys, it looked like a castle. Inside were a number of bunk beds, on which they rolled out their sleeping bags. Soon a huge fire was roaring in the stone fireplace. The Scouts were able to thaw out in front of the fire and cook a hot meal. The cabin seemed a safe and cozy haven.

Later that night, the boys gathered around Katooni beside the fire. In a low voice, he started relating some bit of ancient Indian lore. The room smelled lightly of smoke. The golden glow of the fire made shadows dance on Katooni's lined face.

The Indian spoke about his tribe and the battles they had fought to keep their lands. As the boys hung on every word, he told them about his people's belief that spirits lived in rocks and trees and animals. And then he told them about Sasquatch.

"The Sasquatch never show themselves to men," said Katooni. "They live high in the mountains, away from civilization. But they have fewer places to go now. There are too many people."

"What do the Sasquatch look like?" asked one of the Scouts.

"They are tall, bigger than most men. Hair covers their bodies, and they have a strange smell. They fear nothing. They just want to be left alone. But if you threaten them, they will attack you without mercy."

Another boy spoke up. "Have you ever seen one?"

Katooni looked into the fire. "I have seen their tracks a few times," he said. "The track is like a man's foot, only much bigger, with claws. I have seen the Sasquatch itself, just once. Many years ago, not far from this place."

The boys sat quietly, a few shuddering at the thought of meeting a Sasquatch. Suddenly, a mournful wail from deep in the forest pierced the silence.

"WoooooOOOOOOOOOooooooo."

Katooni sat upright, cocking his head, his hand held to his ear. The Scouts started to murmur.

"Quiet!" commanded the Indian.

"WoooOOOOOOOooooo." The unearthly cry echoed through the night.

"A wolf," said the Indian. "Enough stories. Time to sleep."

The Scouts crawled into their sleeping bags, but it was a long while before anyone could fall asleep.

The next day, the boys had forgotten all about the wolf. They romped in the snow, cut firewood, and cleaned out the cabin. They were so busy they didn't notice that Katooni had slipped away alone.

But by the time of the evening meal, groups of two and three boys were going off in different directions calling for Katooni. They returned at dark. Their leader was nowhere to be found.

The boys ate their supper in silence. Some of the younger Scouts were frightened.

The older boys tried to quiet their fears.

"Katooni knows how to take care of himself," said one. "He'll be back soon."

"Yeah, but why did he leave us alone?" asked another. No one had an answer.

During the evening, the Scouts took turns looking out the window, shining a flashlight into the wilderness. As the sun had set it had begun to snow, lightly at first, but now more heavily. The flashlight beam reflected only the large, fluffy flakes.

In a corner of the room, three of the Eagle Scouts tried to figure out what to do next. The troop had planned to stay in the cabin two nights and one day. They were due to leave tomorrow. Instead, they would have to stay and send out search parties to look for Katooni. But on the following day, they would have to start their hike back. They did not have enough food to stay any longer.

As the boys made their plans, the forest suddenly echoed with the same wail everyone had heard the night before.

"WooooOOOOOOOOooooooooo."

"That doesn't sound like a wolf to me," one Eagle Scout told the other.

"It doesn't even sound like a coyote," replied the other. "It almost sounds . . . human!"

* * * * *

The Scouts broke into search parties the next day. They wandered about the forest all day, calling Katooni's name, but the hunt was fruitless. The snow continued to fall, and by evening nearly a foot had been added to what was already on the ground. The younger boys were clearly worried about Katooni, although they had confidence the Eagle Scouts would get them back home safely.

It was dark when the Scouts were finishing their supper. The snow had stopped, and the sky had cleared. A full moon cast a bluish light on the new-fallen snow.

"WoooooOOOOOOOOooooooo."

The boys froze when they heard the wail. This time, they were sure it was much closer. Too close.

With no warning whatsoever, the door of the cabin burst open. Standing in the doorway was Katooni. His heavy coat was shredded and stained with blood. His face had been mauled. He stumbled weakly and grabbed the door for support.

"Sasquatch!" he groaned. In another moment, he slid to the floor.

Behind him stood the creature itself—tall, covered with hair, and giving off a choking stench!

* * * * *

Three days later, a couple of rangers made it to the cabin on snowmobiles. Alarmed when the boys had not returned, the Scouts' parents had alerted the authorities.

Calling to the boys, the rangers approached the cabin. They pushed open the door and looked around in surprise. The boys' sleeping bags were still spread out on the bunks. Remnants of food lay half-eaten in mess kits. Coats and boots were scattered about. But there was no sign of life. Only a small blood stain on the floor by the door pointed to foul play. The Scouts had simply vanished.

The rangers circled the area on their snowmobiles, but there were no leads to follow—

the snowstorm had obliterated any tracks that might have been there.

Using their mobile radio, they called back their unfortunate news, then prepared to stay the night. The rangers had just finished eating supper when they heard it.

"WooooooOOOOOOOOOOoooooo."

The Night He Came Back

BRIDGETTE loved Billy. But Bridgette's father didn't like the young man one bit. *That boy isn't worthy of my daughter,* he thought. But there wasn't much he could do about the romance except to hope the couple would eventually break up.

But it didn't happen, at least not without a little help.

Bridgette won a scholarship to go to college overseas. But if she went, she would have to be gone for two years. She begged Billy to go with her, but he couldn't afford it. Instead, he gave Bridgette an engagement ring and promised her they would be married as soon as she returned.

Of course, Bridgette's father was not very pleased to learn of the engagement. But his daughter would not be swayed. She left for Europe wearing the ring, while Billy remained in town working in the local factory.

Several months went by. Then one day Bridgette's father received a small package from his daughter. Inside was the ring. The stone had come out of its setting, and Bridgette wanted her father to take it for repair to the jeweler who had sold it to Billy. Now Bridgette's father saw his chance. The next day, instead of going to the jeweler, he went to see Billy.

"I've got some bad news," the father told Billy. "Bridgette wrote me that she's met a young Frenchman and has fallen in love. I'm sorry to tell you this, but she sent me her ring and wanted me to give it back to you."

Billy couldn't comprehend what he was hearing. He looked at Bridgette's father in stunned silence while the older man repeated his message.

"I . . . I don't understand," he stammered. "She said she'd never—"

"I know, son," said the father, trying to act sympathetic. "But she's so young, and so are you. It's hard at your age to know what real love is."

As the boy stared at the ground in disbelief, the old man continued his lies. "Bridgette is terribly upset about this," he said. "She doesn't want you to write or call her ever again. And I think she's right. It'll help you both to get over this. I'm sorry."

The father left Billy standing on the porch holding the broken ring. The young man's hopes and dreams were crushed.

When the father got home, he called his daughter overseas and told her a similar tale. He said that Billy had found someone else, and that he never wanted to see or hear from her again.

At first, Bridgette cried terribly and could not be consoled. But eventually her father convinced her that he had been right about Billy all along. The young man, he said, was no good. Wasn't the fact that he had a new girlfriend proof enough? In bitterness and sorrow, Bridgette came to agree.

And so that was the end of that, thought the interfering parent. But it wasn't long after that Billy got sick and died. Some people said he died of a broken heart. Bridgette's father felt guilty about what he had done, but he didn't dare tell his daughter of Billy's death.

Eventually, Bridgette returned home. She had many stories to tell about her travels abroad, things she'd done, and people she'd met. No one spoke about Billy. His memory was dead and buried.

One night not long after her return,

Bridgette was visiting a friend. A knock came on the door. When she joined her friend to answer the door, Bridgette was shocked to see Billy standing on the porch.

"Bridgette, you have to come with me," he said. "Your father needs you at home right away. He asked me to come and get you."

Not knowing that Billy had died more than a year before, Bridgette walked out with him, got on his motorcycle behind him, and left.

"I thought you didn't want to see me anymore," she yelled over the whine of the engine. "Who is this girl you fell in love with?"

"I've loved only you," said Billy. "I want you to remember that always. Everything else has been a mistake."

As she held onto Billy, Bridgette thought he felt cold and clammy. "Are you okay?" she asked.

"My throat's sore," said Billy. When he stopped the motorcycle at an intersection, Bridgette took off her scarf and tied it around Billy's neck. In a short while, Bridgette was home.

"Father, what's wrong?" called Bridgette as she ran into the house.

"Nothing," he said in surprise. "Why are you home so early?"

"Well, didn't you send for me?"

"No, what for?"

"Billy said you called him to come and get me and bring me home right away."

Bridgette's father turned white. "Billy?" he whispered. "How did you get here, Bridgette?"

Bridgette pointed out the window to the motorcycle parked by the street. But Billy was nowhere to be seen.

Terrified, the old man blurted out the terrible story that he had been hiding for so long. Waves of grief and then of fear swept over Bridgette. Finally, she felt a bit of hope.

"It must be," she decided, "that Billy is not really dead. I know he isn't! I saw him myself!" She ran for the phone and dialed the nearly forgotten number. Billy's mother answered.

"No, Bridgette," she said icily in answer to the girl's request. "Billy isn't here. I can't imagine you would care, but don't you know he's been dead for 15 months?"

But Bridgette could not be convinced that Billy was dead. When it was discovered that Billy's motorcycle was missing from the garage where it had been stored, Bridgette became all the more insistent.

At length it was decided to dig up Billy's grave. It seemed that exhuming the body would be the only way Bridgette would ever be persuaded to give up her useless hope.

The sun shone down on the little group as the coffin was raised from the hole. Slowly, the workmen pried back the lid. It creaked as it gave up its seal.

Inside lay the wasted body of Billy, as neatly laid out as the day of his funeral. Only one thing was different. Around his neck, lovingly tied, was Bridgette's scarf.

The Headless Brakeman

AS a brakeman on the railroad, Joe Kramer never worked long on any one line. Whenever he got bored with the route he was working, he would ask for a different run. Then he'd hitch a ride on a caboose to the starting point of the new job.

So it wasn't unusual that Kramer was bumming a ride one cold, rainy spring night. As the caboose lurched along, he waited for the on-duty brakeman, an old friend of his, to come back from inspecting the cars. *What a miserable night,* he thought as he peered out of the window at the pelting rain. He pictured his friend climbing over the tops of the swaying cars, and he was glad to be safe inside the caboose.

Kramer was slowly nodding off to sleep when suddenly the train jolted violently, throwing him to the floor of the caboose. *A washout!* he thought. *The engine's hit a washout, and I'll bet the whole train is derailed!*

Grabbing a lantern and climbing out of the tilted caboose, Kramer heard the screams and cries of the passengers, but his only thought was of his friend. He searched frantically along the tracks. What he found exceeded his worst fears. Lying between two cars were the grisly remains of his friend's body. And the body had no head!

Kramer and the crew picked up the body and placed it in the baggage car, covering it with a blanket. They returned to the tracks and searched until dawn, but they did not succeed in finding the man's head.

* * * * *

It was a long time before Kramer felt at peace again. But despite the horrible experience, he wasn't tempted to quit the railroad. Trains had always been his love. Eventually he became a fireman, and later he was promoted to engineer. Happy in his new job, he nonetheless tried to avoid taking assignments on the run where his friend had met his terrible fate.

But engineers are not as free as brakemen to take only the jobs they like. Despite his best efforts, the time came when Kramer was forced to make the run. Reluctantly he prepared the engine and picked his crew. They would leave that night at eight.

It was a chilly, rainy evening, much like the night nearly 20 years before that Kramer remembered so well. All went smoothly for a couple of hours. But as the train approached the curve where the fatal washout had been, the engineer glimpsed a faint red light in the distance.

Kramer hit the brakes, and the freight train screeched to a halt. He told the fireman to go out for a look. Kramer was puzzled when the fireman returned, saying no light was to be seen.

"I'll go have a look for myself," he decided. Sure enough, as he jumped down to the track, he distinctly saw a red light swaying in the distance.

Skipping from tie to tie, his own white lantern swinging by his side, Kramer moved forward toward the red light. Soon he could tell it was an old-style, red-globed lantern. It faintly lit up the lower part of a man's body dressed in the regulation blue overalls of a brakeman.

"What's wrong?" yelled Kramer as he approached the brakeman. Getting no answer, he shouted again, but the dimly lit figure only moved away from him further down the track.

Kramer followed, moving his feet uncertainly across the uneven tracks. He tried to keep his eyes focused on the shadowy form in the rain, but it kept slipping out of sight. Then suddenly, it would reappear, just ahead.

An eerie feeling came over Kramer as he followed the figure around the very curve where his friend had died. Rounding the sharp bend, he froze in horror. Covering the tracks was a pile of earth and rocks—the worst washout he had ever seen. And standing atop it was the figure with the red lantern. But now the light was held high by an outstretched arm, and Kramer sensed the truth in the instant before he looked. With a sickened feeling, he saw that the figure had no head! In another instant, the ghostly brakeman was gone.

*　*　*　*　*

Joe Kramer was an engineer for more than 15 years after that, but he never accepted another assignment on that run. Younger engineers scoffed when they were told that Kramer believed he had been saved from disaster by a ghost. But when Kramer died one cool, wet night in the spring, some say you could see two shadowy figures with red lanterns, walking up and down the tracks on the fateful curve. And one of the figures, they say, was headless.

The Viper

IT was well after midnight when Randy heard the knock on his door. He was tired and just about to get ready for bed.

The sweet sounds of Dixieland jazz drifted up to his room from the French Quarter below as he cracked open the door. It was Hannigan.

"Let me in. I have to talk to you," said Hannigan. He looked nervous.

"What about?" said Randy, yawning. "Do you know what time it is?"

"Just let me in, okay?"

Randy shrugged and opened the door. *What could this be all about?* he wondered.

Hannigan plopped himself down on the edge of the bed. Randy took a seat beside a small table in the seedy hotel room. *Geez,* he thought. *What am I doing here in this dumpy place with a half-crazed guy?* Randy hoped his visitor would leave soon.

"You got anything to drink?" asked Hannigan, his eyes searching the room.

"There's a soda in the icebox. Come on, Hannigan, what's up?"

Hannigan walked over to the mini refrigerator tucked under the desk, and pulled out a can. He popped it open, took a drink and then sat down at the table with Randy. As he slid into his seat, he pulled a pistol from his jacket.

"What—what are you doing? What the heck—" Randy spluttered as he stared at the gun that was pointed at his chest. "Hannigan, what's going on?"

"You really thought I was that stupid, huh?" said Hannigan. "The deal comes down, you make off with the money, and we get nothing."

"What are you talking about? I didn't do anything," said Randy.

"Like heck you didn't. Where's my money?"

"I don't have any money. If I did, do you think I'd still be here in this dump?"

"I think you'd do whatever you need to do to look clean. But now all you're going to look is dead!"

"Hannigan, you've got this all wrong. The money wasn't—"

"Shut up!" Hannigan yelled. He rose halfway up out of his seat, then slowly sank back with a sickening smile spreading across his face.

"Shooting you would be too easy," he said. "The police might be able to trace the gun, anyway. No, I've got a better idea."

Hannigan reached into the pocket of his nylon windbreaker and pulled out a little cloth bag. Still holding onto the gun, he carefully opened the drawstring and set the bag at Randy's feet. He dumped its contents onto the floor. It was a little green snake, no more than six inches long.

"A guy at the docks sold this snake to me," said Hannigan, moving back a few steps and brandishing the pistol. "He said they find them on the banana boats. They're supposed to be one of the most poisonous snakes in the world."

Randy sat perfectly still, his eyes wide, intently watching the snake. The little viper slithered closer to his leg, then rose up tensely, ready to strike.

"Hannigan, wait, I know you think—"

Lightning quick, the snake struck one, two, three times. Its razor-sharp fangs cuts cleanly through the thin cloth of Randy's pants.

Randy made no attempt to move. The snake slithered under the bed.

Hannigan grinned again, pleased with the fast

action. "The guy at the dock said it only takes a minute or two, maybe less. I'll stay and watch." He dropped the gun to his side.

Suddenly Randy burst out laughing. Hannigan looked at him, confused.

"Hannigan, I really like you. You're not stupid at all. This is a great plan. But there are two little things wrong with it. First, I didn't double-cross you—Lacy did. He took the money and is long gone. That's why I'm still here."

The other man looked at him suspiciously, his eyes narrowing.

"Second," Randy continued, "that snake isn't poisonous. It's just an ordinary garden snake. Those guys at the docks really put one over on you! I'm not dying—just watch me! Here, grab those cards and we'll play while we wait."

Randy drew his chair up to the table and motioned to Hannigan to sit down. Still eyeing Randy with doubt, Hannigan took his seat again. He slowly cut the cards with one hand while in the other he still held the gun.

As they played, Randy told Hannigan the details of how Lacy had double-crossed them. After two games of rummy, it was clear that Randy wasn't going to die, and Hannigan laid down the gun.

"Sorry to come busting in here," Hannigan mumbled. "Looks like Lacy's the man I have to get."

As he spoke, the snake reappeared from under the bed.

"Look, Hannigan, I'm tired and you did give me a scare," said Randy. "Let's call it a night so I can get some sleep." He promised that they would get together the next day and plan how to get Lacy. Hannigan mumbled another apology and headed for the door.

"Here take your gun," said Randy. "And don't forget the snake. I understand they make great pets. But you have to keep them warm. Just put it in your pants pocket. They love body contact."

As he closed the door, Randy wondered how long it would be before the snake would strike through the cloth of the pocket. He walked over to the bed, reached underneath, and pulled out a briefcase. Opening it, he started counting the stacks of $20 bills.

It was only a matter of moments before he heard Hannigan's screams from the street below. Randy paid no attention, but kept on counting. When he was finished, he slid the briefcase back under the creaky bed. He pulled down the covers and unbuttoned his shirt.

Then, bending over, he rolled up his pant leg and unbuckled his artificial leg.

The Incredible Case of Captain Hanson's Leg

CAPTAIN John Hanson was as good a sailor as you'd ever find. He always took care of his men and his ship, no matter what the danger.

He had lost his leg protecting his crew. Years ago, a fishing expedition had taken them into rough seas, and one of his men had been swept over the side of the ship. Hanson grabbed a line and dove in after him. As he dragged the half-drowned sailor to a lifeboat, a great white shark had risen up from the sea and made a single, devastating attack. When they pulled him out, the sailors found their captain's right leg sliced away at the knee.

Not one to surrender to fate, Hanson immediately got fitted for an artificial leg. But it wasn't just any old peg that he wanted. Hanson ordered a hand-carved, mahogany limb with a little copper boot on the bottom to keep it from wearing down.

And the leg served him well. He wore it proudly for years. He tucked his pant leg in at the knee to show off the gleaming wood below, and he even treated the peg with furniture wax if it got the slightest knick.

Hanson impressed all the ladies with his shark story, but he was even more impressive on the dance floor. To see him jig, you would never have suspected he wasn't born with a wooden leg.

One of the young ladies who caught Hanson's eye was Betty Crofton, the daughter of a whaler who had perished at sea. After a whirlwind courtship, John and Betty were married in the sailor's chapel in the seaport town Betty had grown up in.

The couple never had children, but that was fine with Captain John. His life was the sea. But most people thought he was tempting fate every time he set sail. Sailing folk believe that once a great white shark gets a piece of a man, it's never satisfied until it finishes the job. That shark, they were sure, was just waiting out there for Hanson. But the captain just laughed at such superstition, and continued his life at sea.

It was late November, about Thanksgiving time, when Hanson's ship, the Sea Witch, ran into a powerful gale. It took three days for the heavily damaged vessel to limp back into the harbor, listing heavily to the side. Its masts were bare, for the wind had ripped the sails away. But the worst news that the crew carried was that Captain John and two other men had been washed overboard.

Within a few days the bodies of the two men had drifted ashore. But there was no sign of Hanson. His body was never found. But weeks later, two boys discovered the captain's prize leg, half buried in the sand on the beach.

The crew of the Sea Witch, mourning the death of their captain, cleaned and waxed the peg and presented it to his widow. Grateful for their loyalty, she tearfully accepted their gift. She and the captain had been married for over two decades, and now she found that the mahogany leg gave her a strange consolation. Sometimes at night, she would hold the limb in her lap and speak to it as if it were alive.

More than a year passed after the tragedy. One night near Thanksgiving, Betty went to bed early and fell into a fitful sleep. She awoke with a start to find Captain Hanson standing on one leg at the foot of her bed. He leaned against the bedpost, then hopped over to her side.

"The barometer's falling, Betty, dear," he

whispered, "and we're fixing for a nasty nor'easter. I'll want my leg to keep me steady when the thick weather strikes."

He reached out and pinched her cheek. Betty closed her eyes and pulled away in fear. When she looked up, the vision was gone. She rubbed her eyes. *It must be a dream,* she told herself, and fell back asleep.

The next morning, Betty noticed she had a little red spot on her cheek where her ghostly visitor had pinched her. *It couldn't really have been John,* she thought. *I must have scratched myself in my sleep. But what a real dream!*

Betty went on trying to convince herself that her husband's appearance had been only a dream. But before going to bed that night, she took the skipper's old leg out of her cedar chest. She placed it, polished and shiny, by the fireplace.

As predicted, the terrible storm blew up that night, a nor'easter of powerful proportions. Trees were bent over, ready to snap. Huge waves battered the beach. The wind sounded like the howl of a thousand drowned sailors arising from the deep.

As she tossed in her bed, suddenly Betty heard a thump, thump, thump on the floor of the sitting room downstairs. "It's just my imagination," she breathed to herself as her pounding heart mimicked the noise. In a moment she heard what she thought was the slam of a door. Outside, the wind moaned. Betty slid down under the covers of her bed and moved not a muscle till dawn.

As the pink sun streaked the sky, Betty tiptoed downstairs to see if the captain's leg was still there. It lay as she had left it. But when she picked it up, she found that it was wet.

The woman's mind reeled. *The storm was so bad,* she thought, *that rainwater must have seeped down the chimney, soaking whatever lay near the fireplace.* All morning she rehearsed the explanation. But her fear and worry couldn't be calmed. By afternoon, she had taken to her bed in a cold sweat.

Neighbors summoned the village doctor, who examined her with care. "Nothing's physically wrong," he told her, "but I can see something's troubling you." With a little more persuasion, he coaxed the story out of the woman.

Leaving the bedroom, the doctor went downstairs and examined the wooden leg. A bit shaken himself, he returned to speak to the widow, carrying the mahogany leg.

"Mrs. Hanson, you say you left the leg by the fireplace all night? And the rain came in and it got wet?" The widow nodded silently in reply. The doctor set the peg down, walked over to the bed, and took a firm grip on the woman's arm.

"Mrs. Hanson, I want you to ask one of the men to take that thing out to sea, weight it down with net leads, and heave it overboard."

The widow looked at him in dismay.

"I'm a trained doctor," he continued, "and I don't listen to wild stories. But Mrs. Hanson, I put my tongue to that wood. It doesn't rain saltwater."

The Dog Man

THE gate to the wire mesh fence surrounding the dingy green house on the far edge of town was locked.

"Anybody home?" yelled Bradley from the gravel berm of the road.

Inside the house, a dog barked. Then a second started barking, a third, and a fourth. Suddenly the house exploded and shook with barking. Twenty—maybe 30—dogs filled the air with their howls, yelps, and woofs.

Bradley's knuckles whitened as he gripped the gate. "Anybody home?" he yelled again.

The yard inside the fence was barren. Not a blade of grass could be seen anywhere. As the hot sun baked the red clay, Bradley thought the yard looked like a giant brick.

The visitor waited another few moments at the gate. Still no one came to the door of the house. The deafening sound of the dogs would certainly have aroused anyone inside. And Bradley had no intention of jumping the fence to knock on the door.

But just as Bradley was turning to leave, the door cracked open and an old man slipped outside. Hunched over, he slowly shuffled toward the gate.

Bang, bang, bang!

The dogs were hurling themselves against the house's metal door in an effort to get out. The man approached, seemingly unaware of the fury behind him.

When he reached the gate, the old man stopped and stared at Bradley, his bleary eyes full of curiosity and irritation.

For a moment, Bradley stared back. *So this is the famous Dog Man*, he thought.

"Sir," said Bradley, "I'm here on behalf of the county. According to our local laws, a homeowner can have no more than three dogs living in a single-family residence. It's obvious that you have far more than that." He handed the old man a paper.

"Here is a court order telling you to dispose of all your extra dogs within 30 days. Otherwise, we will have to take them away ourselves."

The old man continued to stare at Bradley as if he hadn't understood a word.

"Listen, mister. Do you know what I just said? You have to get rid of those dogs. People are complaining."

As if they knew what was going on, the dogs began barking even more loudly. Flashes of teeth and fur appeared at the bottom of the front room window. But still the Dog Man did not respond.

Bradley was disgusted, and a little unnerved. "Look," he said, "I've given you the court order. I'll be back in 30 days."

As he turned to walk back to his police car, Bradley thought he heard the old man mumble, "You'll be sorry."

* * * * *

It was only a couple of days later that the police got a report of a dog having bitten a child. Bradley was assigned to investigate.

The stray dog had disappeared, so the little girl was going to have to undergo rabies shots. Bradley felt sorry for the child. He listened closely to her story, hoping it would help him find the animal.

Apparently, the dog had been very friendly to the child. In fact, she said it seemed the dog wanted her to follow it. As the girl and the dog had neared the edge of town, the dog had suddenly turned on her, bit her hand, and tried to drag her along. Luckily, a passing car had stopped and the driver had scared the animal away by hitting it with a tire iron.

Bradley noted that the attack had occurred only a short distance from the Dog Man's house.

Through that afternoon, the case stayed uneasily on Bradley's mind. He kept thinking of the fact that a number of children had been reported missing in recent weeks, and all of them had been from the same side of town. The little girl had spoken of being lured by the dog. Bradley decided to pay the Dog Man another visit.

It was night when he pulled his car up alongside the road a little way from the green house. For some reason, Bradley felt it best not to let the dogs and their master know he was coming.

As he walked up the gravel road, he noticed the beam of a flashlight in the Dog Man's backyard. Bradley stopped and watched intently.

The old man had a bag and a shovel in hand. As Bradley watched, the Dog Man dropped the bag and started digging into the hard clay, making a little hole. Then he dumped the contents of the bag into the hole and covered it over again, packing down the earth.

Bradley walked back to his car and got inside. *I'll just wait until everyone's asleep,* he thought. *Then I'll see what's in that hole.*

A couple hours later Bradley was inside the fence by the freshly dug earth. He dug at the hole with a small camping shovel he kept in the cruiser. In just a few moments he hit something hard.

Turning on his flashlight, he reached into the hole and pulled out what he thought was a large stone. Shaking the dirt off it, he stared in horror. It was a child's skull!

Suddenly, Bradley heard a low growl, then a dog's barking. He had time only to glimpse a pair of yellow-green eyes and a row of fangs before those teeth sank into his upraised arm.

He wrestled with the dog, rolling and kicking. But the vicious dog kept tearing at his arm. Reaching down with his free hand, he was finally able to pull his gun from its holster at his waist. Aiming as best he could as he writhed to free himself, he shot. The animal collapsed, fatally wounded. Bradley ran for the fence.

By this time, all the dogs in the house were in an uproar. They came streaming from the back door, nearly catching the policeman as he scrambled over the fence. Yelping and howling, they leaped in vain at the spot where Bradley had just disappeared.

But suddenly, the pack fell quiet. The old man was shuffling out of the house, holding a rifle. Peering over the fence, he pointed the weapon at Bradley, who lay sprawled on the ground.

"I said you'd be sorry," said the Dog Man menacingly. "Now you've discovered our secret. And we can't have you telling anyone about it."

The Dog Man cocked the gun. Its barrel trembled only inches from Bradley's head.

"When my money ran out, I couldn't buy food for my babies," he continued. "And about that time a little boy wandered into our yard. Well, my babies were so hungry . . . what else could they do? What a juicy morsel that boy must have been! Now my babies won't eat anything else. So I send them out to get their own food."

Bradley stared at the old man in disbelief. Fear for his life gave way to loathing of this man.

The Dog Man's eyes narrowed, his shoulders hunched, and his voice dropped to a whisper. "I bury the bones in my yard," he went on, "so no one will know. But you have found us out. I told you you'd be sorry."

As the old man's gnarled finger twitched on the trigger, Bradley jerked into action, rolling violently out of the line of fire. He came up firing his own revolver. The bullet found its mark in the Dog Man's chest.

In seconds, the dogs were tearing voraciously at their old master's body.

The Terrifying Tale of Taily-po

YEARS ago, an old man lived deep in the dark woods of Tennessee. Because he never came out of the forest, and was never heard to speak a civil word to any human being, the folks around there called him simply "the hermit."

No one could remember the time when the hermit had not lived there. People believed—and they were probably right—that they had better keep their distance from the crusty old man. And no one really cared to visit him in his forest cabin up in the hills. There were legends about that part of the forest—tales of hikers, birdwatchers, and loggers who had headed that way and had never been heard from again.

But the hermit wasn't frightened. He had two big dogs—Shep and Curry—to protect him. He loved those dogs more than a mother loves her children. At mealtimes, the hermit fed his dogs first with the food from his table. Shep and Curry shared the hermit's one-room log cabin, and the old man always let them take the warmest spots by the fire on cold winter evenings.

Never have there been more loyal dogs. Shep and Curry were totally devoted to the hermit, and they never left his side.

One day the hermit and his dogs went fishing at a stream about a half mile away. They were gone for most of the day, and when they returned, the cabin door was open. Inside, everything was a complete mess. Cans of food lay scattered on the floor, furniture was turned over, curtains were torn, and the hermit's homemade banjo was crushed and broken.

The only clue to be found was a single footprint. A bag of flour had been spilled on the floor. The white stuff gave a ghostly coating to one corner of the room. In the midst of the flour was a single white print. Large and beastly, it was unlike anything the hermit had ever seen.

But the hermit wasn't frightened. Instead, he was angry. He was sure that children from the village a few miles away had broken into his cabin, trying to scare him. They could have drawn the strange animal track in the flour.

The hermit set about that very afternoon putting a new and bigger lock on his door.

Several days later, the old man was cooking a stew in the big kettle hanging in his fireplace. It was late afternoon, just starting to get dark. Shep and Curry had gone outside the cabin to play. The hermit hadn't noticed that he could no longer hear their barking.

As he was stirring the stew, the old man heard a scratching on the door. Thinking it was his dogs, he went to let them in. He flung open the door, and jumped back in horror. Before him was a creature about seven feet tall. It stood on two legs and had a face like a man. But it was covered with matted hair, and it had a long pointed tail. Breathing with a heavy, rasping noise, the beast started into the cabin.

The hermit let out a yell and grabbed his ax, which was just inside the door. As the hermit swung the ax wildly, the creature backed off just enough to miss the swoosh of the passing blade. The hermit swung again, and this time he caught the creature's tail against the wall. The sharp blade did its work, and the tail, cleanly severed, fell to the floor.

The creature gave a horrible scream and ran toward the woods. The dogs, returning to the cabin, gave chase and followed the creature into the thicket, howling and snarling viciously. After a while they returned, much to their master's relief.

The hermit was badly shaken. He would have to keep his beloved dogs nearby from now on. Of course, the creature probably wouldn't return. The old man felt sure his loyal dogs had killed it.

As he started to calm down, the hermit looked at the tail on the floor. Not one to waste anything, he prepared the meaty morsel and threw it into the kettle. That night he and the dogs had a fine supper of creature-tail stew.

Deep in the night, all was quiet in the cabin. As the moon crossed the sky and its light broke in through the window, the hermit woke to the sound of scratching at the cabin door. The dogs lifted their heads and growled. *It has to be the creature,* thought the hermit.

The scratching noise moved to the side of the cabin. Slowly lifting the bar, the hermit inched open the door, the dogs at his heels.

"Shep! Curry! Get him!" he cried as the dogs bounded outside and around the corner of the cabin. A terrible howling followed. In the moonlight, the hermit could dimly see the dogs hounding the huge beast back into the woods. As the creature disappeared into the night, the old man heard the howling turn to an eerie cry: "Taily-po, taily-po, all I want's my taily-po."

The next night, the hermit was awakened once again by the sound of scratching at the door. Like the previous night, he sicced his dogs on the hairy intruder, and the tailless creature fled. And again in the night he heard the same voice wailing, "Taily-po, taily-po, all I want's my taily-po."

With a feeling of dread, the hermit lay awake on the third night, knowing the scene would be repeated. Once again, the scratching. Again, the dogs were loosed on the beast. But this time, Shep and Curry did not return. In the morning, the old man found his pets dead by the stream. He looked at their bodies in horror. Their tails were gone.

Heartbroken, the hermit stayed in his cabin day and night, his shotgun by his side. The creature didn't return, but every night he thought he could hear it calling, "Taily-pooo . . . Taily-pooo . . ."

Finally one night, in the early hours just before dawn, the hermit heard the same familiar scratching. But this time the noise was coming from the foot of his bed!

Shaking the sleep from his eyes, the hermit sat bolt upright and found himself staring into the contorted face of the creature.

"Taily-po, taily-po, all I want's my taily-po," moaned the beast, which looked more human than before.

"I don't have it," cried the hermit, his eyes fixed on the creature, while his hand frantically searched for his gun.

"Oh, yes, you do," came the last low growl as the beast, claws extended, sprang at the hermit's throat.

* * * * *

All that's left of the hermit's old cabin these days is the fine stone chimney, standing alone in the woods. But people say if you're up at the old place on a moonlit night when the wind blows from the north, you can hear the same unearthly moan echoing through the forest: "Taily-po, taily-po, all I want's my taily-po . . ."

About the Author

MARK MILLS lives in Worthington, Ohio, a suburb of Columbus, with his wife, Aija, and two children, Ryan and Marissa.

His interest in ghosts began around the campfires of Boy Scout outings when he was a youngster. Although he claims to never have seen a ghost, he does believe some phenomena are unexplainable.

Mark is also an avid sports fan. He enjoys attending sporting events at his alma mater, The Ohio State University, with Ryan.